Soldier

by Kara Van Kirk Levin

illustrations:
Vlada Soshkina and Polina Doroshenko

On a very blue night, in a very old forest, a baby porcupine was born.

His eyes twinkled like diamonds, his ears stood tall and proud, and his mouth was as small as a button.

"I will call him S o l d i e r," his mother pronounced. Just as she said his name, the wind picked up and blew the word through the trees. And liking the sound of his name dancing on the wind, Soldier smiled at his warm and gentle mother.

His smile made her so happy that
she opened her arms to hug him, but she could not.
Something was different about Soldier.
"Mama, **what's wrong with Soldier's quills?**" his brother
and sister asked. "Why won't they lie flat?"
"I do not know," she said as tears welled in her eyes.
And at that moment, Soldier's eyes went dim, his ears turned down,
and his little button mouth grew smaller.

And time passed, and Soldier grew, and still, **no hugs**.

Wishing to cheer him up, Soldier's father whittled him **a wooden flute.**

Every night **Soldier climbed to the top of the tallest tree to play his special flute.** The sound was like the wind itself, dancing and gliding through the forest night. And all below would listen, as the music put them softly to sleep.

One night, a field mouse with busy hands and smart eyes
heard the beautiful but sad music.
"Tomorrow night I shall find this music-maker," she said to herself.
The following night she waited. With the sound of the first note, she set off
in the direction of the music.

At last she came to the tallest tree and at the very top could see a small figure with a little wooden flute. So up she climbed. Soon she was close enough to realize the problem.

"Oh, I see," she thought to herself.

"This little porcupine cannot be hugged."

Just then she had an idea and hurried home.

The next morning, she called upon her friends and asked them to listen.
"I know who makes the beautiful music that dances on the wind," she announced.

"And I know why it sounds sad. He is a little porcupine and

he needs our help."

She instructed the animals to go to the dressmaker's cottage and explained that there they would find a pile of leftover cotton scrap. She asked them to return with the cotton and to be certain to bring her the strongest pieces they could find.

FREE
-LEFTOVERS-

The animals wasted not a moment. They gathered as much strong cotton as they could carry and returned before nightfall.

Next, they waited as the mouse began to work. And work she did, all night long and into the next morning. When finally she emerged, there before them was **the most beautiful sweater** the animals had ever seen.

"Now," said the mouse as she examined the extra thick sweater, "this should do the trick." And at nightfall she set out once again to find the music maker.

Beneath the tree she waited until Soldier appeared. "Hello, my friend," she said.
"Your music is the most beautiful we in the forest have ever heard, and for that
I have come to thank you and to offer you this gift."

"**Please**," she said gently, "**try it on**." Soldier's heart began to race.
He had never seen a sweater like this before.
Nervously, he pulled the sweater over his head. To his surprise, it snapped firmly
into place. Then, Soldier did something he had not done in a very long time.

He smiled.

Soldier glanced in the direction of his home. "Go to them," said the mouse. "They will want to see you." With his excitement growing, he took several steps toward home then remembered something. He turned to the mouse and in his bravest voice said, "Thank you."

Soon he arrived home and there waiting for him, as she did every night, was his mother.

"**Mama**," he said with a twinkle in his eye, "**now will you hug me?**"

"Soldier!" she cried. Without waiting another moment, she threw her arms around him.

His father joined, as did his brother and sister,
and **they hugged him for** what seemed like **days.**

And from that day on, the music that filled the forest night was no longer sad but more beautiful than ever.

The end ♪♫

To James,
with whom the beauty of our childhood resides

First edition 1000 books 2016

Library of Congress Control Number 2016901998
ISBN: 978-0-9972558-0-5

Printed in Kiev, Ukraine

This book was typeset in Monotype Walbaum™ Pro Medium
Book design by Ira Gvozdyk

LiTTLE WOODEN FLUTE

2016 published by Little Wooden Flute
Brooklyn, NY

visit us at littlewoodenflute.com